I dedicate this book to my grandson, Grayson.

To Aaryn and Franc
You are what is special about February 2nd!

Grayson's Adventure Begins on Groundhog Day!

Hello! My name is Grayson.
I'm four years old.

Something special is about to happen, I'm told.

The sun waves from the sky above and brings a smile to my face.

I see a giraffe, a frog,
and a man from outer space.

In the kitchen I smell something sweet.
A symphony of scents dancing around my nose
is such a treat.

Something special is near the hour.

Daddy's face is still covered in flour.

Streamers hanging as a vibrant chandelier.

Balloons galore seem to appear!

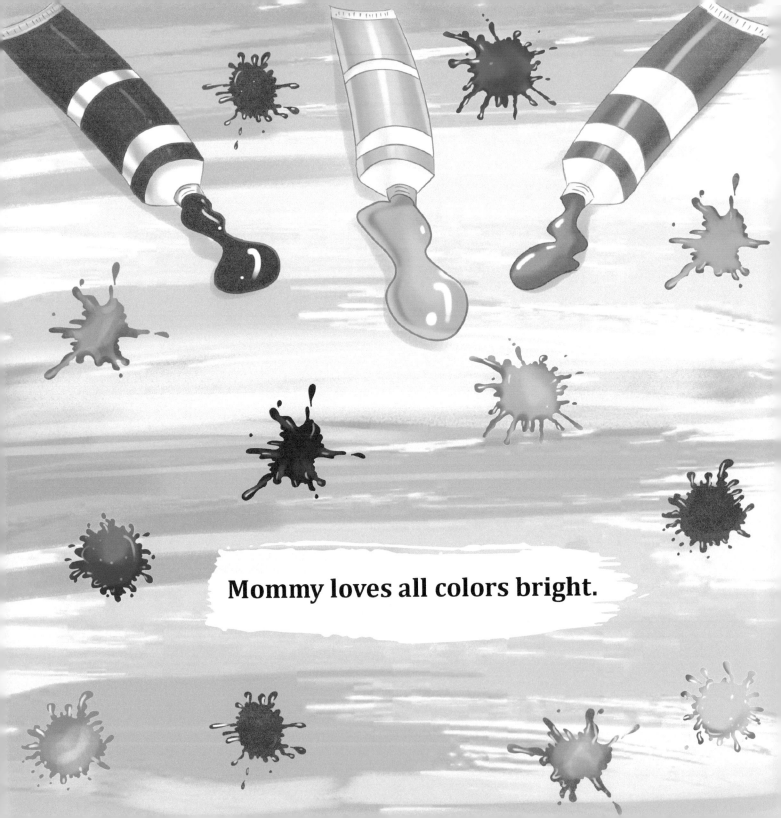

Mommy loves all colors bright.

Add RED and GREEN, a pinch of WHITE.

What is special about today?

We must work fast while Mommy is away.

Daddy, what is special about today?
Is it when the groundhog finds his way?

With a thump of his paw he makes his choice.
He'll face the sun and raise his voice.

No more hiding, no more sleeping.
It's time for spring, the groundhog is leaping!

Shh! What's that sound I hear?

HAPPY BIRTHDAY

Do you know what is special about today?

These pages are for you to color.

Groundhog Day is recognized on February 2nd, when the groundhog comes out of its burrow. He will decide the weather.

ONE!

TWO!

THREE!

These pages are for you to color.

Made in the USA
Columbia, SC
30 December 2024

48720130R00015